First Flight
80 003 217 445

Sch

Titles in More First Flight

Comic Chaos	Jonny Zucker
Into The Deep	Jonny Zucker
Cyber Phone	Richard Taylor
Mutt	Jane A C West
Captured!	Alison Hawes
Robot Goalie	Roger Hurn
Alien Eggs	Danny Pearson
Just in Time	Jane A C West
The Speed Flyers	Jonny Zucker
Super Teacher	Stan Cullimore

Badger Publishing Limited
Suite G08, Business & Technology Centre
Bessemer Drive, Stevenage, Hertfordshire SG1 2DX
Telephone: 01438 791037 Fax: 01438 791036
www.badger-publishing.co.uk

Captured! ISBN 978-1-84926-454-9

Badger Publishing would like to thank Jonny Zucker for his help in putting this series together.

Publisher: David Jamieson
Senior Editor: Danny Pearson
Design: Fiona Grant
Illustration: Aleksandar Sotirovski

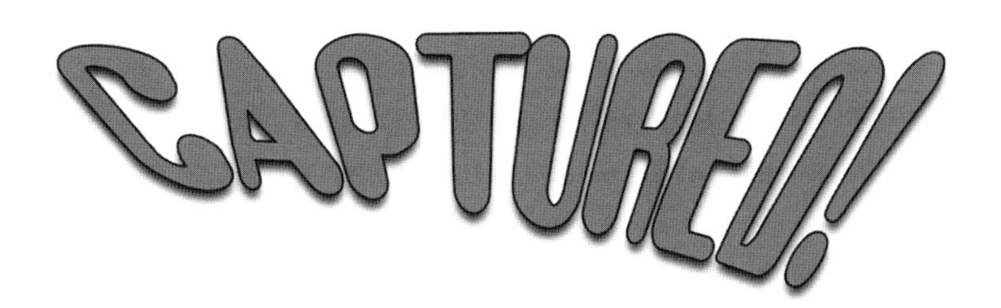

Contents

New words:

pirate	prisoner
corridor	ordered
crawled	straight
guard	rescue

Main characters:

Chapter 1
Captured!

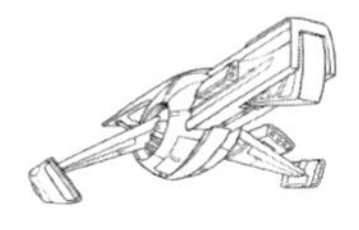

There was a loud crash, then a dull thump!

The small spaceship rocked and shook.

Rob and Lucy were thrown across the flight deck.

"What was that?" they yelled.

"Hold on tight!" said Mike. "We've been hit!"

"I'll go and check for damage," said Jan.

"No!" said Mike. "Don't go outside. It might be pirates."

"Space pirates!" said Lucy. "What would space pirates want with a small spaceship like this?"

"If it's Zanna and her pirates," said Mike. "It's us she wants, not the ship. She will keep people prisoner, until a ransom is paid."

There was another thump and then a hiss as the air locks on the outside door opened.

Jan checked the screens.

"It is Zanna!" she said. "And she's coming this way!"

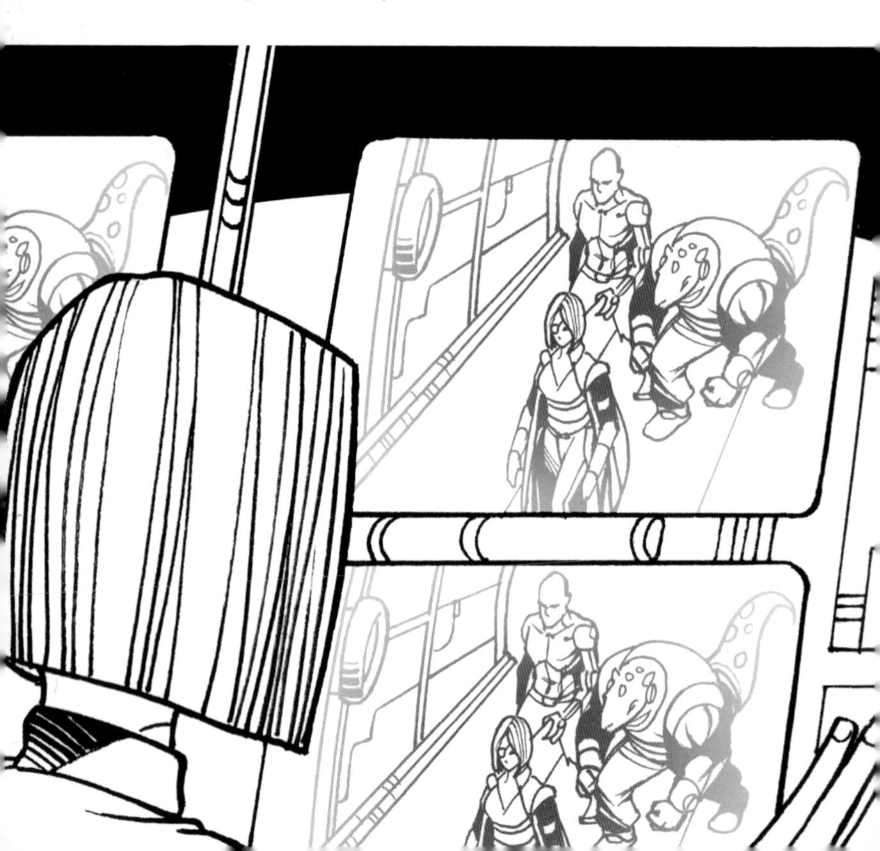

“Quick!” Mike said to Rob and Lucy. “You two, hide.”

“Where?” Lucy panicked.

“I know!” said Rob, and pulled Lucy down the corridor.

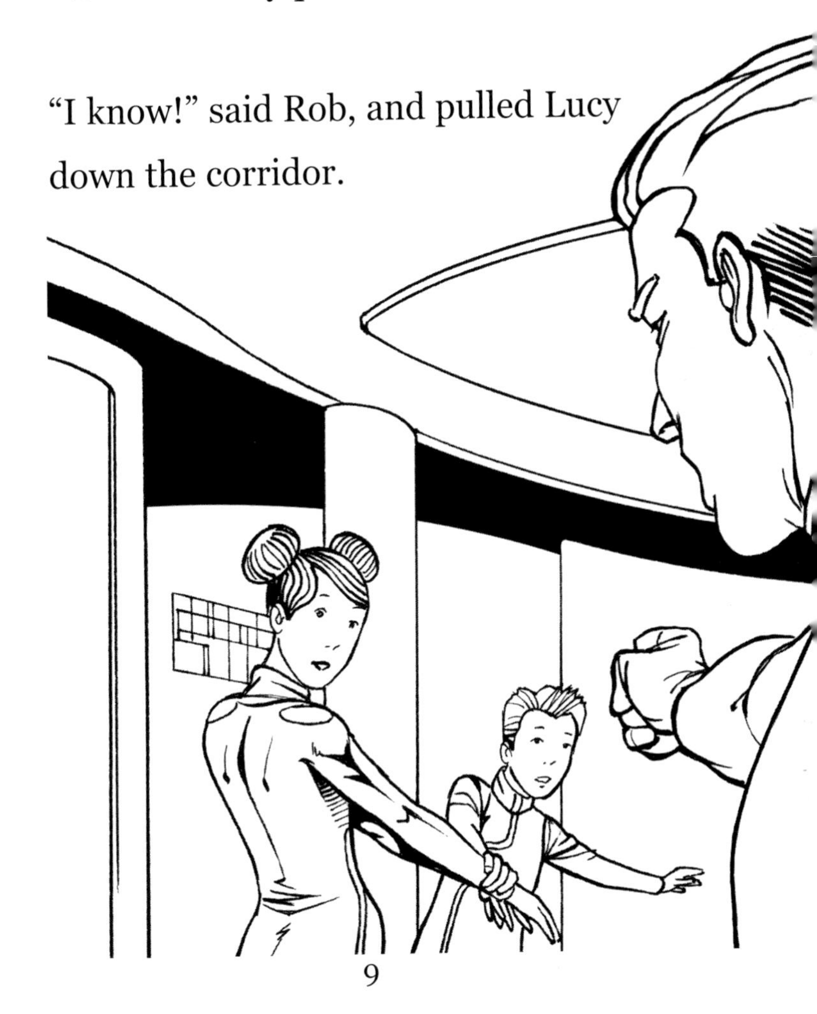

Chapter 2
Hidden

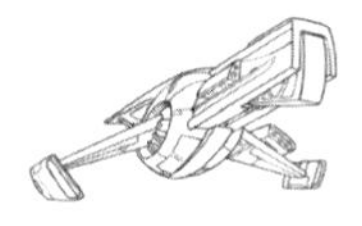

“Quick in here!” Rob said, opening the hatch to the air ducts.

Lucy froze. “I can’t go in there!” she said.

“Hide or be taken prisoner,” said Rob. “But be quick. I can hear the pirates coming down the corridor!”

Lucy crawled inside the air duct and Rob pulled the hatch shut, behind them.

“What now?” whispered Lucy.

“We keep going, until we get to the flight deck,” said Rob.
“Then we can see what’s going on.”

Chapter 3
Out Of Air

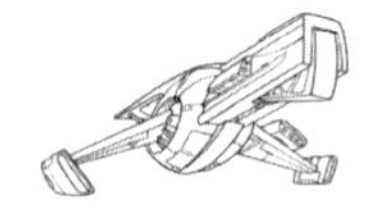

Rob and Lucy looked down, onto the flight deck.

Mike and Jan had been tied up.

“Lock the prisoners in the sleep bay.” Zanna ordered. “And DON'T let them out!”

The pirates nodded and marched Mike and Jan down the corridor.

“Now what?” whispered Lucy.

“First we get rid of Zanna, then we rescue Mum and Dad,” said Rob

“But we can’t fight Zanna!” said Lucy.

“No,” said Rob. “But we can shut off the air to the flight deck.”

"Without air, Zanna will soon pass out," said Rob.

"But she could just open the flight deck door and let air in," said Lucy.

"Not if I go and lock her in from the outside!" said Rob.

Chapter 4
Tricked

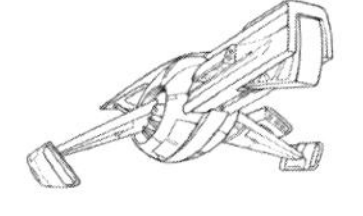

Before long, Zanna began to feel hot and sleepy.

She tried to open the door to let in some air. But it was locked, locked from the outside.

She banged on the door.

She called to the pirates.

But they couldn't hear her.

Zanna was furious. She made her way back to the flight desk.

Fighting for air, she just had time to reset the computer, before she passed out.

Inside the air duct, Rob and Lucy heard Zanna slump to the floor.

“Quick!” said Rob, “let’s rescue Mum and Dad. Then they can tie Zanna up, while she’s still unconscious.”

“But what about the other pirates?” asked Lucy.

“I have a plan,” said Rob. “But you will have to pretend to be Zanna!”

“No way!” said Lucy.

“But you must,” said Rob. “It has to be a girl.”

Rob and Lucy crept down the corridor towards the sleep bay.

Rob peered round the corner.

The pirates were on guard, outside the door.

"Come on, Lucy," said Rob. "We must do it, now!"

Lucy froze. "I'm scared!" she said.

"I know," said Rob. "But it's the only way to help Mum and Dad."

Lucy nodded and followed Rob back down the corridor and unlocked the flight deck.

Zanna was still slumped on the floor.

Rob stood on guard, in the doorway, while Lucy went to the desk and pushed a switch.

She took a deep breath.
"Pirates to the flight deck, NOW!" she ordered, trying to sound like Zanna.

For several seconds nothing happened.

Then Rob heard the sound of running feet.

"Quick, come out of there!" said Rob. "They're on their way!"

Chapter 5
Too Fast

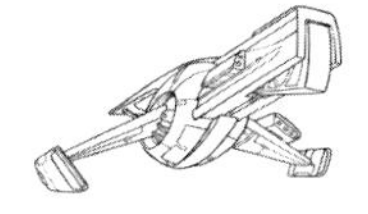

As soon as the pirates ran onto the flight deck, Rob and Lucy locked them in, straightaway.

“I’ll stand guard,” Rob said. “You go and get Mum and Dad.”

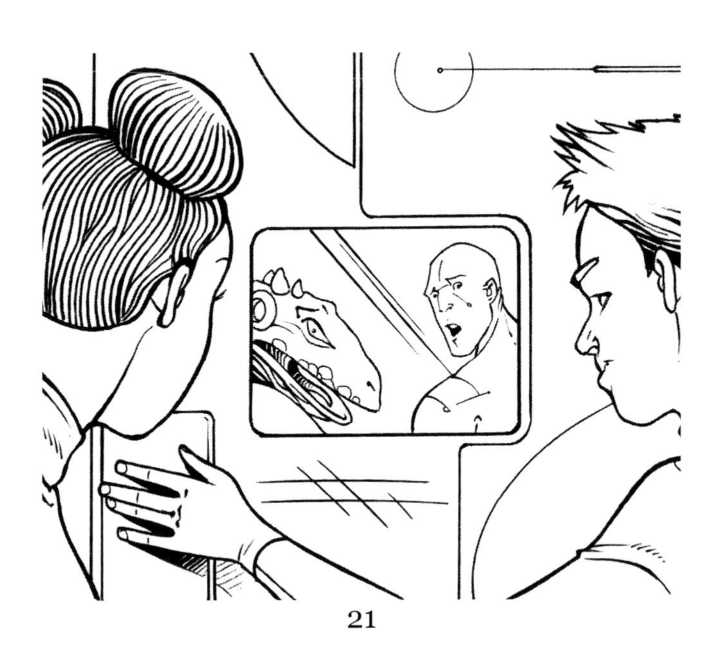

Lucy untied her Mum and Dad and minutes later, they joined Rob outside the flight deck.

Mike peered through the window. "You two go and open the air duct and your Mum and I will tie up the pirates," said Mike.

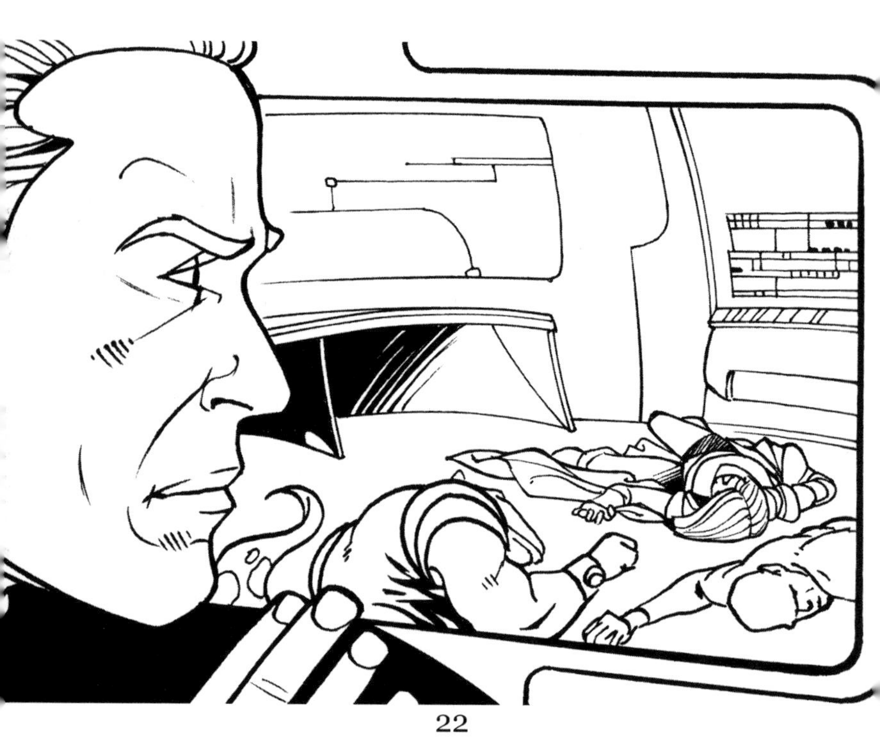

Before long, the pirates began to come round.

“We’re on our way home,” Mike said to Zanna. “And when we land, we’re handing you over to the Space Police.”

Zanna laughed. “I don’t think so!” she said. “Have you checked the flight computer?”

Jan checked the screens. “We’re heading straight for our planet,” she said. “But we’re going far too fast.”

Zanna began to laugh.
“If you don’t slow down, you’ll crash!”

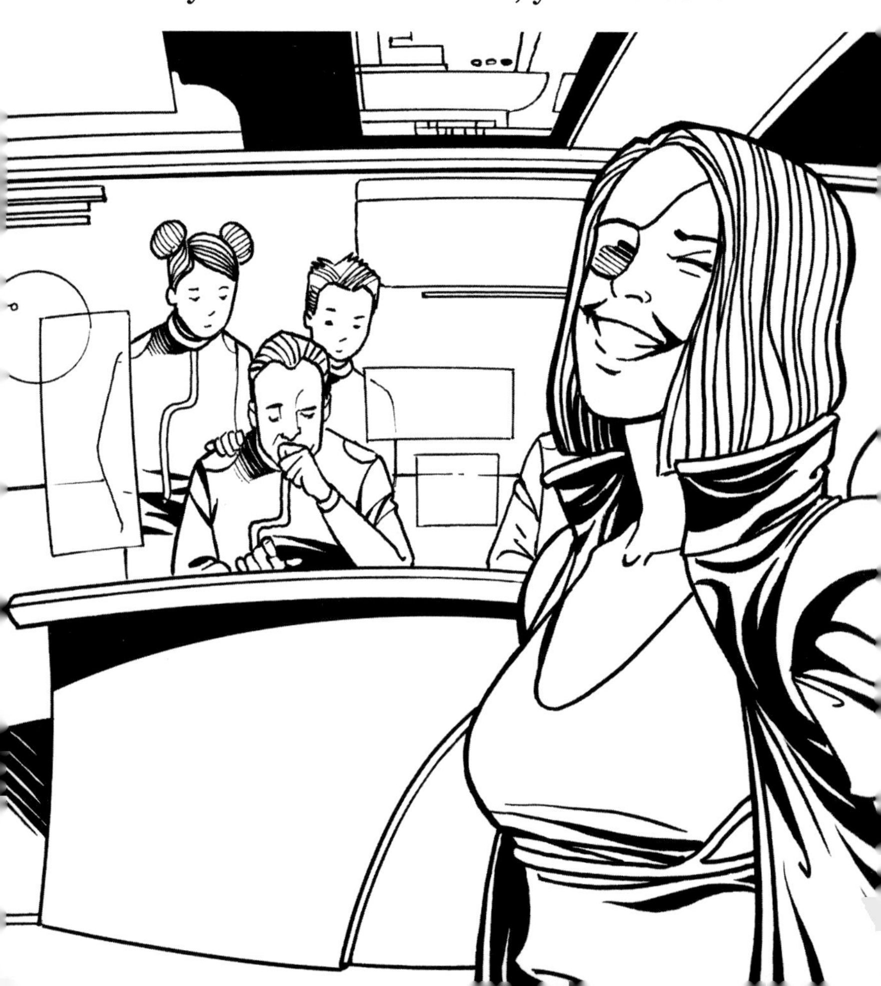

Chapter 6

Crash Landing

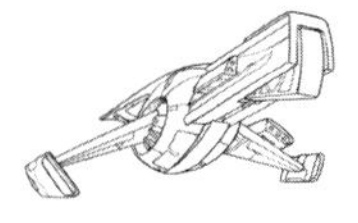

The spaceship was closing in on the planet.

“The computer won’t let me slow down!” Mike said.

“I told you!” laughed Zanna.

“So what can we do?” Lucy panicked.

There’s only one thing we can do,” said Mike. “We must switch off the computer and land the ship without it.”

"But you haven't done that since Space School!" said Jan.

Mike took a deep breath. He switched off the computer and took over the controls.

The spaceship slowed but was still going too fast.

He pulled the ship hard right, just missing the spaceport roof.

"Hold on." he said, "We're coming into land!"

There was a loud crash.

The spaceship rocked and shook.

Rob and Lucy were thrown across the flight deck.

"What was that?" they said.

“That was how not to land a spaceship,” laughed Mike.
“I need to go back to Space School!”

"But first," he said, looking straight at Zanna. "I need to take you three to the Space Police."

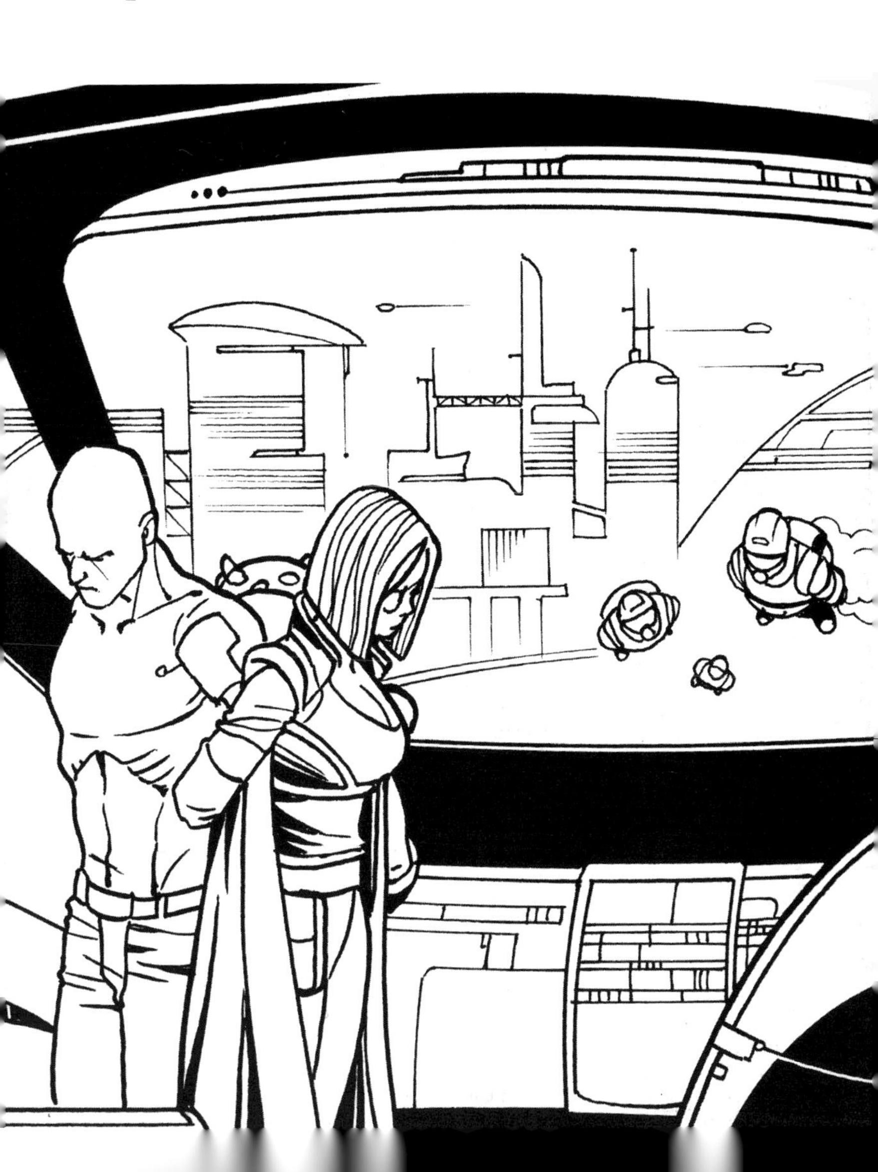

WANTED

Charlotte De Berry

Born: England 1636

Her Crimes

Charlotte married a sailor and dressed as a man so she could go to sea with him.

But when she was captured by pirates, she took over the ship and became a pirate captain herself!

WANTED

Rachel Wall

Born: America 1760

Her Crimes

Rachel and her husband stole a ship and used it to capture other ships.

They pretended their ship was in trouble. Then they robbed the ships that came to help them. Then they sank them!

Questions

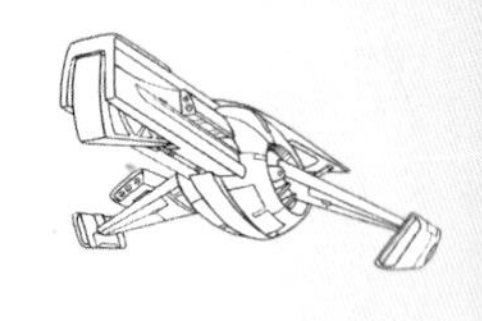

- *Who was Zanna?*
- *How did Rob and Lucy overcome Zanna?*
- *How did Rob and Lucy trick the pirate guards?*
- *What had Zanna done to the flight computer?*
- *What did Mike have to do to land the spaceship?*
- *What do you think happened to the space pirates in the end?*